# THE SECRET-KEEPER

# THE SECRET-KEEPER

story by
Kate Coombs

paintings by

Heather M. Solomon

Atheneum Books for Young Readers
NEW YORK   LONDON   TORONTO   SYDNEY

Atheneum Books for Young Readers

An imprint of Simon & Schuster

Children's Publishing Division

1230 Avenue of the Americas

New York, New York 10020

Text copyright © 2006 by

Kate Coombs

Illustrations copyright © 2006 by

Heather M. Solomon

Book design by Abelardo Martínez

The text for this book is set in Jante.

The illustrations for this book are

rendered in watercolor, oil, and collage.

Manufactured in China

First Edition

10 9 8 7 6 5 4 3 2 1

Library of Congress Cataloging-in-

Publication Data

Coombs, Kate.

The secret-keeper / Kate Coombs ;

illustrated by Heather M. Solomon.—

1st ed.

p.    cm.

Summary: The people of Maldinga

and the surrounding area bring their

deep, dark secrets to Kalli, who keeps

them all safe until they become too

much for her to bear.

ISBN-13: 978-0-689-83963-4

ISBN-10: 0-689-83963-4

[1. Secrets—Fiction.

2. Villages—Fiction.]

I. Solomon, Heather M., ill.

II. Title.

PZ7.C8115Se 2005

[Fic]—dc22    2003024695

*For my dad, Robert H. Coombs,*

*who believed in me*

*—K. C.*

*For Adam*

*—H. M. S.*

Kalli was the secret-keeper of Maldinga.

Every day the people of Maldinga straggled through the woods to the clearing where Kalli's cottage stood. They came one by one, never in twos or threes. And one by one, they told Kalli their secrets.

Early one morning, Sheld the baker came to the cottage. He gave Kalli a basket of fresh rolls and a copper coin. Then he whispered, "I sell loaves weighing less than full measure." Kalli nodded and caught his words in her hand.

After Sheld trudged away with a sigh, Kalli opened her hand again. Sheld's secret was a small gray rock, like a stale bread crumb. Kalli went inside and tucked the secret into one of the hundreds of tiny drawers that lined the walls of her cottage.

Another day, when the sun was high and hot, Relsa the marriage-maker hobbled between the trees to Kalli's door and babbled, "Kalli, I've made a bad match. He has a cold heart, but he paid me so well that I married him to the nicest girl in Maldinga!"

Relsa thrust a great skein of yarn at Kalli in payment and turned to go. As the old woman hurried away in the heat, her secret became a tin heart in Kalli's hand. Kalli slipped the secret into a drawer and set herself to weaving.

The next evening Went, a rich farmer, knocked at Kalli's door. "Kalli," he said gruffly, "last winter a beggar came to my house and I turned him away. Maybe he died in the cold." Went pulled a silver coin from a pouch at his fat side and dropped it into Kalli's hand.

Her other hand held the secret. After Went lumbered off, Kalli opened her fingers and stared at a second silver coin, a coin with no face.

There were so many secrets.

A small boy didn't like his new baby sister.

The grocer's wife had hidden ten gold pieces under a tree root.

A plain girl loved a handsome boy and dared not tell him.

The miller's son had stolen a coat.

The tailor had left his widowed mother alone and come to Maldinga to seek his fortune.

The mayor's daughter was sneaking about, keeping company with a young rascal.

And so it went—day in, day out. The villagers, folk from neighboring towns, and even a few strangers from farther away came to the clearing in search of the secret-keeper. Then they went away, a little lighter of heart.

By and by, all of the villagers had come to talk to Kalli, some more than once. All, that is, except Taln, the potter's son. He sold her two plates painted with spring flowers. But he never came to Kalli's door with a secret.

The secret-keeper found herself returning to the potter's shop. The other villagers smiled politely and edged away whenever they saw her in the square. Only Taln spoke to her, asking Kalli whether she liked summer best, or fall; if the blackberries had ripened in the woods; if she had seen the traveling players' puppet show.

Kalli bought a green bowl with a goblin face and a pitcher the color of a lake in autumn. She couldn't imagine anyone without a secret.

The red and yellow leaves fell, catching in Kalli's hair as she walked back
and forth to the village. Then came a long, dark winter. When the snow was
still thin and the sun sometimes shone, the villagers bundled up and trudged

out to the little cottage to murmur their secrets in clouds of breath. When
the snow grew deep and the wind bayed through the village, they huddled
beside their fires, hoarding their secrets till spring.

The secret-keeper had always liked winter with its blue shadows. But this year she began to shiver and cough. Days passed, and the snow melted at last. Still Kalli lay in her bed counting secrets, growing pale and sad.

The village folk began to tramp through the mud to knock on Kalli's door again, but there was no answer. . . .

Until, one morning, a young girl was bold enough to turn the door knob and step into the cottage. She came thumping back to the village square with the news that Kalli was very ill. Word spread quickly, and the villagers hurried along the path into the woods to find out what ailed their secret-keeper.

For the first time they came to Kalli's home in groups of two and three, whispering worriedly. They brought her bread and soup, clustering in the cottage and the clearing, but when they asked her what was wrong, Kalli was silent.

Finally, old Relsa spoke. "Kalli, we've told you our secrets—please, won't you tell us yours?" Kalli sighed, a sigh like all the sighs the villagers had left in the clearing outside her cottage. Then she whispered, "The secrets are so heavy. Dim and dark and sad, like a child lost in the snow."

The people of Maldinga were astonished. They peered at one another, picturing mysteries. A goodwife spoke up. "Comes of living all alone in the forest."

Kalli shook her head. "I like the forest."

"Take a journey," Sheld the baker suggested. "See the great city of Porthl."

"No," Kalli answered slowly.

"Perhaps," said the blacksmith, "if we shared some secrets now—together."

The villagers flushed and muttered.

"Good secrets," the smith added hastily.

The mayor cleared his throat. "Are there no good secrets for Kalli? Bright and fair secrets, like a spring morning?"

Everyone was quiet for a moment. Then a boy stepped closer to Kalli and said shyly, "I haven't told anyone yet. I'm going to be a painter when I grow up."

His mother squawked, but his father shushed her, and when Kalli opened her thin hands, a butterfly with blue wings flew past the villagers into the matching sky. Kalli smiled.

Heartened, the villagers pressed forward. The innkeeper's wife said, "Not a soul knows it, he's that quiet, but when no one's looking, my husband helps folks." The innkeeper's face turned poppy-red, but Kalli's hand freed a meadowlark.

An ancient man creaked up with his wrinkled wife by his side. "I married my own true love," he said stolidly. She laughed like a child, hugging him as a rainbow fluttered out the window like a bouquet of flowers.

"I made up a song," said a cowherd. A purple dragonfly rode the breeze.

"My mama and I dance in the meadow," blurted a little girl. A green frog hopped zigzag through the morning grass.

"I run my business fairly," Sheld told the secret-keeper.

"That's no secret!" called a farmer. But Kalli nodded, spring leaves lifting from her hand into the cool air.

Then a young wife said softly, "I'm going to have a baby," and Kalli held a robin's egg while the young husband twirled his wife into the clearing. So each of the villagers came forward, filling the morning with laughter and springtime.

But they fell silent when the last of their number, Taln the potter's son, slipped through the crowd to Kalli's side.

"You're here," she said, puzzled.

"I have a secret," Taln told her. He looked into Kalli's eyes and whispered, "I love the secret-keeper."

When Kalli opened her hand, she held a sunrise-colored rose.

Then how the people cheered! The butterflies wove through Kalli's clearing, and everyone ate bread and soup and told jokes and sang songs and hunted violets till sundown.

Well, Kalli is still the secret-keeper of Maldinga, still filling tiny drawers with sorrows. But she shares her cottage with her husband, Taln, and one morning every spring the villagers gather in the clearing to give her their happiest secrets.

Then the butterflies pinwheel in the spring air as the villagers dance, while their children pick violets and the sunrise-colored roses that grow all around Kalli's cottage.